Giddy Goat

In loving memory
of John and Ruth
J.R.

For Robyn and Tilly
L.C.

ORCHARD BOOKS
96 Leonard Street, London EC2A 4XD
Orchard Books Australia
32/45-51 Huntley Street, Alexandria, NSW 2015
1 84121 424 8
First published in Great Britain in 2003
Text © Jamie Rix 2003
Illustrations © Lynne Chapman 2003
The right of Jamie Rix to be identified as the author and
Lynne Chapman to be identified as the illustrator
of this work has been asserted by them in accordance
with the Copyright, Designs and Patents Act 1988.
A CIP catalogue record for this book is available from the British Library.
2 4 6 8 10 9 7 5 3 1
Printed in Belgium

Jamie Rix

Lynne Chapman

Giddy Goat

ORCHARD BOOKS

In a land above the clouds, perched between Heaven and Earth

on top of a bare and rocky mountain, lived a family of goats.

These were no **ordinary** goats.

These were rock-climbing goats,

with hooves that clung to cliffs like sticky socks.

These were acrobatic goats that could

leap

plunging
ravines
while the
toy-town
world
buzzed
below.

These goats knew no fear.

Except one.

Giddy Goat was the
youngest of the kids
and had no head for heights.
Stand him on a ledge and his
knees would turn to jelly.

"Make the spinning stop!" he would cry, clinging to the rock face.

Giddy Goat didn't feel like a mountain goat at all.

One day, the family took a picnic right to the top of...

The Needle!

Giddy was so terrified that he couldn't move a muscle.

"Come on, Giddy," pleaded the other kids, "we haven't got enough players for Rock Rounders."

"Then play something else," quivered Giddy.

While the other kids played Catch Tag, Giddy pointed to the lush, green meadows below where the sheep grazed.

"I want to live down there," he trembled, his tummy tumbling like a butter churn.

"With the Muttons?"
said Pa Billy. "Never!
You're a goat, Giddy!"

"Muttons can't even
climb molehills!"
said his mother.

But that night, Giddy Goat ran away from home.

He strapped himself to a tea tray and tobogganed down the mountain with his eyes tightly shut.

In the morning, when he opened them again,
he was upside down

in a low-lying meadow where the woolly wimps grazed.

"I've come to be a sheep," Giddy said
to a wrinkled ram called Ramilles.

The old ram stared at Giddy
with eyes as cold as marbles.
"You're a smelly goat," he
said. "We're far too good
for the likes of you."

"Sheep and goats don't
mix," said the old ram.
"Go home, goat!"

Poor Giddy crept away from the flock and cried.

How could he go home, when
home was twenty thousand feet off
the ground and he was **scared of heights?**

Suddenly, he heard a noise.

It was a faint far-away bleating that whispered through the clouds.

It was the sound of a new-born lamb lost on the mountain.

Giddy knew how frightened
that lamb would be. He knew
it would fall unless rescued. He
also knew that only he could help.

Giddy had to find the fearless goat inside himself!

He tiptoed up to the mountain and placed a hoof on the steep path.

Stones crumbled underfoot.

But it was now or never!

With one fearless **bound** Giddy sprang on to the rock face.

He bounced from boulder to boulder,

and flew over ravines like a great bearded bird.

Giddy was climbing!

He found the lamb trapped on a narrow ledge.
"Hello," he said. "I'm Giddy."
"So am I," trembled the lamb,
who was called Edmund.
"No, Giddy's my name,"
chuckled the goat. "What
are you doing up here?"

The lamb
looked sheepish.

"I want to be a rock
climber," he said.
"Really?" said Giddy.
"Follow me!"

Giddy started to climb. 'Do exactly what I do.'

In no time
at all Edmund was
skittering up and down the
mountain like a full-time goat!

Giddy's brothers and sisters couldn't believe their eyes. "You climbed The Needle!" they gasped.

"Me and Edmund," said Giddy.

"But he's a weedy Mutton," said his kid sister.

"Is he?" said Giddy.

It didn't take
Edmund long to prove that he had a knack for climbing.
And with two extra players, they
finally played that game of Rock Rounders.
They had so much fun that

they didn't notice that the sun was going down...

until
Edmund
heard his
mother
calling.

Edmund was so tired that Giddy
lifted him onto his back and
carried him home, skipping down
the mountain as sure-footedly
as any mountain goat had
ever done before.

The sheep gave Giddy a hero's welcome for rescuing Edmund. Ramilles said that now Giddy could live with them in the valley.

"You're very kind," said Giddy, "but I think it's time I went home, don't you?"

"Giddy, will I ever see you again?" said Edmund. "Of course," said Giddy. "I'll see you in the morning."

So every day as the sun spread its fiery fingers across the valley,

Edmund and Giddy met halfway up and halfway down the mountain to play games.

Some nights they would sleep over.

"Giddy," said Edmund one night, "now that both of us can live in the valley and climb mountains, are we sheep or goats?"

"Neither," whispered Giddy. "You and I are special, Edmund. We're friends!"

And with smiles on their faces, they both fell asleep.